I celebrated
World Book Day 2022
with this gift from
my local bookseller

and Hachette
Children's
Group

D0177459

Other books starring
Bubbles the guinea pig:

THE WIZARD IN MY SHED

THE WARRIOR IN MY WARDROBE

WORLD BOOK DAY

World Book Day's mission is to offer
every child and young person the opportunity
to read and love books by giving you the
chance to have a book of your own.

To find out more, and for fun activities
including our monthly book club, video
stories and book recommendations, visit
worldbookday.com

World Book Day is a charity
funded by publishers and booksellers
in the UK and Ireland.

World Book Day is also made
possible by generous sponsorship from
National Book Tokens and support from
authors and illustrators.

First published in Great Britain in 2022 by Hodder & Stoughton

1 3 5 7 9 10 8 6 4 2

A CIP catalogue record for this book
is available from the British Library.

ISBN 978 1 444 96447 9
EXPORT ISBN 978 1 444 96448 6

Typeset in Archetype
Printed and bound in Great Britain by Clays Ltd, Elcograf S.p.A

The paper and board used in this book
are made from wood from responsible sources.

Hodder Children's Books
An imprint of
Hachette Children's Group
Part of Hodder & Stoughton
Carmelite House
50 Victoria Embankment
London EC4Y 0DZ

An Hachette UK Company
www.hachette.co.uk

www.hachettechildrens.co.uk

THE WIZARD AND ME

MORE MISADVENTURES OF ~~MERLYN THE WILD!~~

BUBBLES THE GUINEA PIG

ILLUSTRATED BY CLAIRE POWELL

SIMON FARNABY

HODDER

People and animals you will meet in
my very exciting story.

BUBBLES: ME!
Best Guinea Pig Ever

ROSE:
Best Owner
Ever

MERDYN:
Most Annoying
Wizard Ever

BOB:
Most Barky,
Bitey Dog
Ever

SNOTTY KID:
Snottiest Human Ever

CATRINA, ANDREA AND TAMSIN:

Mean Girls

DAY 1

Hello?! Is this on? Right, good. Hello!! This is an historic day in history. Possibly the most historic day of all time. I, Bubbles, a guinea pig, have been given the power of speech, thanks to a pine cone around my neck. (More on that later, it's complicated.)

OK. So. My owner, Rose, has given me a

Dictaphone, which is a voice-recording device I'm speaking into right now.

One day in the future, someone will find this Dictaphone and write down what I'm saying and make it into THE BEST BOOK PROBABLY ACTUALLY EVER. How do I know? Listen, I've SEEN books, OK, they are mostly BORIIIIING! This one will not be boring. It will be the greatest book OF ALL TIME!

I would write my amazing book myself but Rose won't let me touch her laptop because last time I tried to use it I did a wee on it and she had to take it to the computer shop to get it mended. She's lucky I didn't do any poos as wees and poos tend to happen close together.

Oh, oops! I hadn't meant to talk about wees

and poos. Sorry. Let me get to the point of my very important story …

Actually, before I do that, I just want to say ONE thing about wees and poos. I'm a guinea pig. Guinea pigs wee and poo A LOT. Nearly ALL THE TIME. It's just a fact. WE DON'T DO IT ON PURPOSE, OK? We eat food, drink water, and then we wee and poo – it's called biology, GET OVER IT! Right. Enough about wees and poos.

So. Wow, what a day I've had! I've seen actual magic happen! I've met a real wizard! And I've added him to my list of things I hate:

1) DOGS. I HAAAATE DOGS!

2) BEING HUNGRY.

3) WHEN MY CAGE GETS TOO FULL OF POOS.

4) DOGS.

I KNOW I'VE SAID THIS ALREADY BUT I HAAAATE DOGS.

HAAAATE THEM.

5) MERDYN THE WILD.

(THE WIZARD I JUST MENTIONED.) OR ANYONE ELSE WHO TRIES TO EAT ME.

Rose and I met Merdyn the wizard in the wood. It was after she came home from school with water leaking from her eyes again. Can I just ask, why do humans leak water from their eyes? What's that all about? Is it wee? Do humans WEE from their eyes?! Anyway, whatever it is, Rose does it. A LOT.

She didn't used to. It started when her dad went away and then she had to go to this new school.

Now look, I understand that she might have some human problems that I'm not aware of, but whatever they are, when she got home today I had a bigger problem … I WAS HUNGRY!! So, I got up to the bars of my cage and scratched on them. She noticed me, bent down, opened the cage and picked me up.

"Oh, Bubbles," she said. "You trying to cheer me up?"

I wanted to say, "No! I'm starving!" but I couldn't speak at this point, so she couldn't hear me.

Then I tried to ask her for some food WITH

MY EYES. I do this
by straining really
hard and making
my eyes go really

big. Sadly, doing this face sometimes leads to a
poo dropping out of my bottom which is what
happened then. The poo landed on a map and
somehow Rose took this as a sign to RUN
AWAY FROM HOME!

The next thing I knew, she was packing a
bag and I was like, OK, if we're running away,
just don't forget to pack my food. All the time
when she was packing, I was staring at my jar of
food, stretching my eyes at it. Looking at Rose.
Looking at the jar. Looking at Rose, looking at
the jar. But I got nothing but three more poos

escaping from my bot-bot.

Before I could say, "THE FOOD, YOU DOPE!!" we were out the door and in the middle of some woods and Rose hadn't got a clue where we were. I could tell she was regretting running away. She sat down, opened her bag and said, "Oh dear, Bubbles, I forgot to pack your food."

I looked at her and I was like, I KNOW!!!!! But just then something happened that scared me so much I immediately and completely emptied my bottom of poos. A MAN WAS FOLLOWING US!

The chap started talking to us. He said his name was Merdyn the Wild and started banging on about being a wizard. Rose and I didn't believe him. Then this Merdyn fella grabbed hold of me and said he was going to EAT ME!! What the HECK?

Rose stopped him from killing me – she shouted, "This is my pet!" – which I suppose I should be thankful for. I mean, I will NEVER forgive her for forgetting my food. But I DO thank her for saving my life.

The mad bloke didn't give me back to her though. He threw some PLANTS over me, said some mumbo-jumbo words and pressed a pine cone to my head. I was thinking, *Get off me, you weirdo!* At that point, the strangest thing that's EVER HAPPENED to any animal IN THE WORLD happened. I started to hear my thoughts OUTSIDE my head. And let me tell you, when you're an animal and you hear your voice OUTSIDE your head, you REALLY feel the need to do a poo. *IneedapooIneedapooIneedapoo!* I thought and then I heard it outside my head. "IneedapooIneedapooIneedapoo!"

I had a VOICE!

Rose heard it, Merdyn heard it. I was now a TALKING GUINEA PIG!

"Go ahead," the wizard said. "Say something else."

"Er ... I don't know what to say," I said.

"What have you always wanted to say to me?" Rose asked.

"Er ... I'm hungry!" I said.

The pair of them burst out laughing, which I thought was very rude, so I decided not to speak for a bit.

Merdyn said he was going to grant Rose a wish. He asked her what she most wanted in the whole of her life and she said, "Well, I want to be a singer, but I'm already a good singer, so I won't wish for that."

Rose, I thought, *You are NOT a good singer. Most of the time, I think you are shouting in pain.*

"That's very hurtful, Bubbles," Rose said back.

Oh. My. God, I thought. I'm going to have to be careful what I think now if people are going to hear me.

When we got home, Rose persuaded her

mum to let Merdyn the Wild stay in our shed. Her mum said she knew him. Humans are a mystery.

We finally came upstairs and Rose gave me some food and water. BETTER LATE THAN NEVER!!! She also tied my pine cone around my collar so that I can talk when I want to. Then she gave me this Dictaphone and now here I am talking to you.

That was my first diary entry EVER! I think it's pretty blooming good. It's possible that there's too much talk about poos and wees, but whoever listens to this and turns it into a book might just leave those bits out so I'm not going to worry about that.

DAY 2

This morning Rose went to school and I made a list of good things I was looking forward to saying now that I can talk:

1) I CAN ASK ROSE FOR FOOD.

2) I CAN TELL ROSE WHEN I NEED THE POOS CLEANING OUT OF MY CAGE.

3) I CAN TELL ROSE WHEN I FEEL POORLY AND NEED TO GO TO THE VETS.

4) I CAN ASK ROSE FOR SPECIFIC TYPES OF FOOD. LIKE AUBERGINE OR CARROTS.

5) I CAN ASK FOR MY FAVOURITE FOOD FROM THE PET SHOP.

All that thinking about food made me feel hungry and it hadn't been long since Rose had left for school. Her mum and brother, Kris, were out too, which left only me in the house.

The mixture of hunger and boredom and being able to speak gave me the urge to make a big and bold decision. I WOULD GO TO THE PET SHOP TO GET SOME FOOD!

Now, I know what you're thinking: Bubbles, aren't you in a cage? But have you SEEN guinea pig cages? They are sooooooo easy to get out of. You just reach up and unclick the fastener to the door. Usually I don't bother. I mean, why would I? I have everything I need in my cage – food, water, some bedding to wee and poo on. I've got a big exercise wheel, although I don't use that. What's the point? You run and run and get NOWHERE!

So I unclicked the fastener, went downstairs, climbed up to the letterbox, pushed my way out and landed on the front path. Easy peasy. But that was the end of the good news. Because there on the front lawn next door was Bob the dog. And I had to GET PAST BOB TO GET TO THE PET SHOP.

Bob is a very nasty dog who always tries to bite my bottom. Did I tell you how much I hate dogs? I HAAAATE THEM. I really do. But now I can speak, which made being outside a MILLION times better.

I would tell you what type of dog Bob is, but I DON'T CARE. He's a dog, OK? A big brown one. A big brown one with a slobbery mouth and wet nose.

What is it with dogs and wet noses? Why is it so wet? What is it? Wee? Do dogs wee out of their noses? I have a nice dry nose, AND dry poos for that matter. Have you smelt dog poos? They are disgusting. The smell is so bad, it's like my nose is on fire! Look at my poos. Small.

Oblong. Dry. And look at dogs' poos. Huge, splodgy, wet! DIS. GUST. ING!!!

So there was Bob, sitting on the lawn with his tongue lolling out of his mouth like a big fish. Sniffing the air with his wet nose. Guarding his precious house. If this was any other day, as soon as he saw me, he would bark and try to bite my bot-bot. But NOT TODAY! Today he wouldn't see me. He would HEAR me!

I cleverly hid behind the

bin at the front of our house and shouted, "Bob! Oh, Bob?!"

Bob's stupid ears pricked up.

This was going to be FUN with a capital F.U.N! Next I went, "Bob! Oh, Bob?! Come here, boy! I've got a treat for you!"

He looked this way and that and sniffed the air. He had no idea where the voice was coming from. He started barking. "Woof! Woof! Woof!" At NOTHING! "Woof! Woof!"

His owner, Steve, a human version of Bob, shouted from inside the house, "Shadapyastoopidog!!"

I felt I was getting close to my goal, so I called again, "Bob! Bobby!"

"WOOF! WOOF!" He was really angry now. A bit freaked out, too. He started snarling and going round in circles. "Grrrrrrr!"

"BOB!!" Steve was getting angry too. "SHADAPAYAGOBYADAFTMUTT!!"

Bob shut up. Whined a bit. Then I did a "Meeow." Like a cat. I'm a genius sometimes. "Meeeow!"

Bob was off again. Twice as loud, barking at the air. "ARF! ARF! ARF! ARF!"

"Right! That's it!!" said Steve and he waddled to his front lawn. "Get in here, you stupid dog. Get in here!"

As Steve shooed Bob in the door and slammed it shut, I came out from behind the bin and walked across Bob's vacant lawn. Inside the house, Bob put his paws on the windowsill and barked through the window. "ARF! ARF!"

"Down, Bob!" shouted Steve. "What's

wrong with ya, boy?!"

I just waved at him and shouted, "Bye, Bob!!"

"ARF! ARF!"

Ha ha! Stupid Bob. And if you thought that was fun, wait till you hear what happened on the way to the pet shop. Hang on though, I need a poo break.

DAY 2 – PART TWO

THE PART AFTER THE POO BREAK

Right. Poo done. So to get to the pet shop I jumped on the number 27 bus, just like Rose does. Unlike Rose I didn't pay! It's amazing how no humans look at the floor when they're walking around. I can scamper about the place pretty much undetected.

I sat under a seat behind this posh

businessman with a moustache wearing a fancy shirt and tie. He didn't notice me 'cos he was talking on his phone.

It's usually five stops to the pet shop so I started counting. After three stops an old lady got on and sat on the seat directly above me, behind the businessman.

Then she put a big plastic box with a cage-like door on the floor next to me. Inside the box was a black and white cat with a cone on its head, obviously off to see the vet. Now, I don't hate cats as much as dogs. I mean, I couldn't possibly hate ANYTHING more than dogs.

Problem is, I might not hate cats – but they sure hate ME! To them, I'm just a big mouse. And they HAAAATE mice.

"Hisssssss," it said like a snake and arched

its back.

"Ah, shut up, Whiskers!" I said quite loudly.

"I beg your pardon," said a voice above me. It was the businessman! He thought the old lady was talking to him!

The cat hissed at me again.

"Shut your mouth, Furry Face!" I said to it. The businessman turned around to look at the old lady again.

"Look," said the businessman. "Moustaches aren't to everyone's taste, but I would ask you to kindly keep your opinions to yourself!" Then he went back to his phone.

The old lady looked confused. She obviously hadn't got a clue what he was talking about. The cat hissed again and tried to swipe a paw at me between the bars of the cage door, but it couldn't reach me because of the stupid cone around its neck, which bumped against the cage.

"Serves you right for wearing that big daft collar!" I said.

The man turned around to the old lady again. "I'll have you know, this shirt is very expensive. It's from Savile Row." He huffed. Then he got off the bus in a right strop.

Oh wow, I was thinking. Talking was going to be GOOOOD!

When I got to the pet shop I snuck inside. There was a man with a beard ordering food for his cat. He was reading from a piece of paper.

"And two tins of Kitty Cat," he said, and the shopkeeper lady went scurrying off to get the food, saying, "Two tins of Kitty Cat" to herself before finding them and putting the tins on the counter.

A plan was starting to form on how I could get my food! The next time the man ordered something, I would add a little request of my own.

"A bag of fish sticks," ordered the bearded man.

"And a box of deluxe organic guinea pig muesli!" I said, trying not to let the bearded man hear me.

"Fish sticks and a box of deluxe organic guinea pig muesli," the shopkeeper said before getting the items.

IT HAD WORKED! YES!

The shopkeeper came back with the goods and put them on the counter. As soon as she did, I jumped up and pulled the muesli down under the counter. I opened it immediately and started eating.

"And a box of Whiskers biscuits," said the beardy man. He was still looking at his shopping list.

"And a box of Whiskers biscuits," repeated the shopkeeper.

"And a pack of Tasty Treats For Rodents!" I said, my mouth full of muesli. My cheeks were so stuffed they were like two giant cheeky pillows.

"And a pack of Tasty Treats For Rodents. Certainly, sir," she said and started to scurry off again. But this time the man STOPPED HER IN HER TRACKS!

"What did you say?" the beardy man said. My heart started beating in my ears – had I been rumbled?

"I said, 'Certainly, sir'," the lady said, before hurrying off.

Phew, I think-said.

The lady came back and put the Tasty Treats down on the counter. I climbed up and grabbed them while she was totting up the beardy man's bill.

"That'll be £29.28," she said.

"Blimey!" said the bloke, putting his cat food in his little bag on wheels. "This stuff's getting expensive."

About ten minutes later I'd finished all my treats and thought I'd better go home. I could hardly MOVE I was so full. I was trying to imagine how many poos all this food was going to be converted into and I just couldn't. So many poos cannot even be imagined!

I looked to see if the coast was clear, waddled out from behind the counter and across the floor of the pet shop when suddenly DISASTER STRUCK!

The first sign of the disaster was when I heard a little boy's voice saying, "I want that one!" The second sign was when I looked up and saw a kid with a snotty nose pointing at me. The third sign was when his mum PICKED ME UP!

It all happened so quickly I didn't know

what the HECK was going on. But when I looked back, I saw that I'd been standing right next to the "Guinea Pigs For Sale" cage!! I knew the cage well because once I'd been in it before Rose rescued me.

"Aw," said the mum, patting me on the head. "He must have fallen out of the cage. Are you sure you want this one, Damien?"

"Yes," said the snotty-nosed kid. "I like him 'cos he's big and fat like Daddy!"

I couldn't believe my undersized ears. Not only was I being kidnapped, now I was being insulted too! The boy plonked me on the counter and the shopkeeper looked at me.

"Ooh, we had a yellow one like this a while ago, but I thought we sold him!" she said.

I wanted to say, "You did sell him, you

idiot!" but if I'd spoken, they would have realised they had the world's first talking guinea pig in their hands and I'd have been sold to a freak show or put on TV. I tried to clear all the thoughts from my mind in case they slipped out by accident.

The shopkeeper lady said I cost five quid. FIVE QUID?! I thought that was cheap, but then she changed her mind and said actually, they could have me half price because I looked like "an old one"! So I cost TWO POUNDS FIFTY. Bouncing bananas! How cheeky is that? That's cheekier than my MUESLI-STUFFED CHEEKS!

Then we went outside and got in the car and I sat with the kid in the back seat. The kid was gripping me tightly. He kept wiping his nose with his hand then drying it on me. So I was COVERED in the kid's SNOT! Did his mum not have any tissues??! What the HECK!

Anyway, I tried to forget I was covered in kid snot and concentrated on my escape plan. I had spotted there was a little gap in the window next to the snotty kid and when his mum pulled to a stop at the traffic lights, it was time to put my plan into action.

I turned to the kid and whispered, "Get your filthy dirty hands off me, you snotty-nosed human."

There was a pause while the kid's eyes grew as big as elephants' feet, which was followed very quickly by the loudest scream I've ever heard in my life.

"WAAAAAAAAAAAAAAAAH!!!"

went the kid.

Snot SHOT OUT of his nose and into my face.

"WHAT THE HECK?!" I screamed. That was not part of the plan. I needed to pull myself together … Ah! The window!!

I leaped for the glass. BUT–

Bzzzzzzzz!

The mum had spotted me trying to escape and had buzzed it up.

"Oh no you don't!" she shouted. "I just paid for you!"

I had to get to the window-buzzing button. I jumped into the front and on to the mum's lap.

BEEEEP! went the horn as she flapped to catch me.

But she couldn't get enough purchase on my snotty fur. Serves her right for not wiping her kid's nose, if you ask me!

"Come here, you!" she said, trying to grab me.

"I don't want him!" the boy screamed. "HE'S A HAUNTED PET!!"

BEEEP BEEP!

Flap flap! went the mum's arms. I was clambering all over the steering wheel, setting off the windscreen wipers, the indicators, the headlamps, the lot.

The traffic lights had gone green and the cars behind were beeping now. The windows in our car were steaming up with all the mayhem. I thought I'd be trapped for ever in this steaming-hot car with a mad mother and a screaming kid when suddenly the door opened and a POLICE OFFICER was standing there!

"Everything all right, madam?" he said. I saw my chance and BOLTED between his knees and RAN as fast as my one-centimetre-long legs would carry me.

I got home, climbed through the letterbox, ran upstairs into my room, climbed into my cage and rolled up into a cosy ball.

There I stayed, shivering for ages.

Hang on. I need a drink of water after all that.

DAY 2 – PART THREE

THE PART AFTER MY MUCH-NEEDED DRINK OF WATER

I stayed in my cosy ball until I heard Rose come up the stairs into my room.

"Wow, what a day I've had!" she said. "Poor you, Bubbles, stuck in here all day."

"Yeah, poor me!" I said. I suppose I could have told her about the exciting day I'd had but I wanted her to keep feeling sorry for me so that she'd feed me.

I didn't need feeding as I'd eaten my body weight in muesli and treats three times over at the pet shop. But that's not the point!

Did she feed me, though? No! Instead she told me all about her amazing day. About going to the library with her new best friend, Merdyn the Wild. How he'd destroyed the place and they'd been chased out by a guard, and how Merdyn had magicked his mouth closed and how then they had seen a poster of the wizard's arch-enemy from long ago on the side of a bus. Weird or what?

When she finished, I said, "Well, that certainly sounds fun. Thanks for the invite!"

"Oh, sorry!" she said. "I didn't think to invite you."

"No. You didn't think, did you?" I said.

"Tell you what. How about I feed you and then you can come downstairs, spend the night with us. We're going to have a sofa night."

"Fine," I said.

So. I stuffed myself with food. Again. And now I am just waiting for Rose to come back in. Ah. Here she comes now. I'll let you know how my evening on the sofa goes later. Bye for now.

DAY 2 – PART FOUR

THE PART AFTER THE SOFA NIGHT WITH MERDYN AND ROSE

Well, that was a very interesting night. It involved some of the best moments of my life. Also, THE WORST MOMENTS OF ALL TIME! I'll do a list at the end so you can see where they ranked.

Rose came upstairs to get me after we'd both eaten dinner and that's when she noticed I was covered in child's snot.

"What's this gooey stuff?" she said.

I didn't want her to get suspicious, so I said, "It's not snot!" But because I said it very quickly, it sounded like I'd said, "Snot's snot."

"Whose snot?" she said.

I panicked and said, "Er … mine."

"Oh dear," she said. "Well, I'd better give you a bath."

Rose took me downstairs and gave me a nice hot bath in the kitchen sink. *NICE*, I thought. If it results in a bath every time, I'll get covered in snot more often!

So the bath was one of the BEST moments ever. But it was followed by one of the WORST.

Merdyn came into the kitchen just as I was getting out. Rose was about to towel me dry as usual when Merdyn stopped her.

"Nay, Rose," he said in his annoying Shakespearey voice. "Alloweth me!"

Then he said a spell – "Holcus Polcus, Blowthewindblow!" – and pointed his finger at me.

Well, knock me down with a giraffe if WIND didn't come out of the end of his spindly finger. REAL. ACTUAL. WIND. It was like he had a hairdryer up his sleeve and it was blowing air out of his fingertip.

It was HORRIFIC!

There was nothing I could do or say as the cold (yes, COLD) breeze blasted my fur this way and that. I genuinely thought he was going to blow all my fur off and I was going to be naked from now on like one of those nude cats.

My cheeks blew out exposing my teeth like tiny piano keys. My eyelids stretched back over my eyeballs like something I saw in a cartoon once. And NOT a good one.

When he finally stopped buffeting me with his windy finger, I looked like a big ball of fluff. Rose tried not to laugh but I could tell she was laughing by the way her shoulders were shaking. The wizard was laughing too.

And I think that was his intention

ALL ALONG.

"I hate you both," I said and left it at that. If this is what life is going to be like living with a wizard then I hope he doesn't stay very long. I don't care if he can make me talk. I am NOT the punchline to a joke. I looked like a cream puff! Don't YOU laugh either, reader … it WASN'T FUNNY, OK?

As we watched a Harry Potter film, me sitting next to Rose looking like one of Rose's grandma's balls of wool after the cat's played with it (I mean it. STOP LAUGHING!), I made a list of all the worst moments in my life to see how the magic-finger-blasting by Merdyn compared. So, starting with the least worst:

5) WHEN BOB THE DOG BIT MY BOTTOM.
(THIS SEEMS TO BE HIS FAVOURITE PART OF ME. WHEN WE FIRST MOVED HERE, HE BIT IT ALL THE TIME!)

4) WHEN ROSE FORGOT TO FEED ME WHEN SHE RAN AWAY FROM HOME.

(SEE DAY 1.)

3) WHEN ROSE PUT ME IN A PLASTIC BALL. WHAT IS THE POINT OF THOSE BALLS?

2) WHEN I GOT KIDNAPPED AND COVERED IN SNOT BY THAT KID.

1) WHEN THE STUPID WIZARD MERDYN THE WILD BLEW ME INTO A HAIRBALL!!

But the crazy wizard wasn't finished yet. While we were watching Harry Potter, he kept shouting at the TV. Apparently, he found it totally unrealistic. At one point he got so angry with what he called "the PREPOSTEROUS names of the characters like DUMBLEDORE!" Did he think Merdyn was a normal name? I suppose I can't talk either. He got so angry that he kicked the TV over and it broke. Rose's mum and Kris were not amused, but I was, because Merdyn hurt his foot when he did it and hopped around the living room going, "Ooh ooh ooh!"

Once he'd calmed down, he said, "We're going to have entertainment Dark Ages style," and he took us into the shed, lit some candles and made everyone tell stories from their life.

Now I must admit, I thought I'd rather spend two hours in a plastic ball than sit listening to everyone tell actual, literal stories from their real lives. But, believe it or not, I quite enjoyed it. Merdyn told a good story about his arch-enemy, a Vandal called Vanheldon. Apparently Vanheldon HATES Merdyn, HAAAATES him. (I wonder why?)

Then Mum told a story, then Kris, and then Rose told hers, which did something very strange to me.

It was a story about how these bullies at school, Catrina, Andrea and Tamsin, had tricked her. They'd rigged her locker so that when she opened it, a bucket of SLIME landed on her head. She turned around and everyone was laughing at her as the green goo trickled down her freckly cheeks.

The strangest thing happened just as she was finishing the story. I was thinking about Rose and what a great owner she is and how she rescued me from that pet shop that day and how she always tries to feed me on time (even though she sometimes FORGETS) and she gives me lots of cuddles. And I was thinking someone like that shouldn't get slime in their hair and have people laugh at them. I was thinking these thoughts when all of a sudden, my EYES STARTED LEAKING.

What's going on? I wondered as I tasted the fluid and realised it wasn't wee, but a salty liquid.

Merdyn must have heard me and leaned in to whisper to me. He had watery eyes as well. "It means you care for her, furry one."

Well, this was NEWS TO ME.

Huh, I thought. *I care about someone. I CARE about Rose.* And you know what?

It feels good.

I've been speaking all this quietly as Rose is asleep now. I'm going to sleep soon too. But stay tuned for tomorrow's diary entry. I'm going to school with Rose tomorrow. And I've got a cunning plan to get revenge on those bullies.

Until tomorrow, my friends!

DAY 3

What. A. DAY.

Rose put me in her backpack with some hay and some food pellets and told me NOT to speak today. If she got caught with a guinea pig at school, she would get into BIG trouble.

It was the first time I'd been to school with Rose and I must say, I was not impressed AT

ALL. First, there was this thing called MATHS.
BORING! Just numbers and stuff. I tried to
listen but none of it went in. Then there was
FRENCH, which wasn't even in the same
LANGUAGE that I speak. Note to self: school
sucks eggs and you LEARN NOTHING!

At lunchtime I couldn't help but notice that
everyone was sitting in big groups except Rose.
She was sitting on her own table. Then I noticed
the mean girls. They were sitting on a table next
to Rose, throwing FOOD at her and laughing.
Rose was trying her best to ignore them as little
green peas ricocheted off her hair and glasses.
She didn't say a word, but I could tell her eyes
were about to get *très* wet with tears. (*"Très"*
means "very" in French. Huh? Maybe you DO
learn something in school?)

Anyway. I wanted to teach those mean girls a lesson and now was my chance. I unzipped Rose's rucksack and poked my head out. I looked left and right to check that the coast was clear before jumping out. I scurried under the mean girls' table. There, as I had hoped, were their three school bags.

I made some quick calculations. I hadn't had a poo or a wee for the last hour, which meant I had at least twenty-seven poos and three wees stored up and ready to go. I did some further maths and realised if I was to dish these out fairly, there was enough to put nine poos in each of the mean girls' bags and one wee in each … Hey! That's pretty good maths! Note to self: you DEFINITELY learn something in school!

I climbed in the first bag and did a wee

in there. I made sure I got it all over an apple and a wafer biscuit. Then I shot out the poos like a machine gun. PHUT! PHUT! WHUP! WHUP! BANG! BANG! PHUT! WHOP! BOOM! Scattering the little pellets from my bot-bot all over the bag.

Then I hopped into the next bag and did the same – Pssst! went the wee, all over some marshmallow sweets.

BANG! PHUT! WHUP! BANG!

went my poo bullets.

I made sure to get some on a hairbrush. (Yes, I know. DIS. GUS. TING! But I was doing this for Rose, OK?)

Next was the third bully girl's bag. I jumped in and did my wee, getting it all over some books and a nice fluffy pink pencil case which REALLY soaked it up. I was midway through shooting my poo bullets when something VERY BAD happened.

"Tamsin, your dad's here to take you to the dentist," said a teacher.

Tamsin picked up her bag with ME IN IT! And SLUNG IT OVER HER SHOULDER! AND WALKED OUT!

I mean, how unlucky was THAT?! As I was carried out of the dinner hall, I could just see Rose through the gap in the zip.

"Rose!" I shouted. "Help!"

But she didn't hear me. My pine cone had fallen off in the bag! My voice was just a squeak again!

OH *MON DIEU*!!!

I couldn't believe I'd been kidnapped AGAIN! I mean, I wasn't even trying to get myself some food or anything this time. I was on a mission FOR ROSE. To get revenge on those mean girls. Because I CARED about her. If this is what happens when you care about someone, I wish I didn't.

What happens next is pretty exciting. But I'm going to need a wee before I tell you. It's THAT exciting.

DAY 3 - PART TWO

THE PART AFTER DOING A WEE

Tamsin met her dad at the school gates and off they went to the dentist. It was across the other side of the park and they were walking there.

I tried to get out, but the zip only worked from the outside. I was trapped! The only escape route was a tiny hole at the base of the bag. It was enough to fit my bottom into but not much else. I couldn't squeeze my little legs through no matter how hard I tried. How the HECK was I going to get out of there and back to Rose?

Then, a miracle.

I heard Steve shouting for Bob.

"Bob! Here, Bob!"

I looked out of the hole. Sure enough, there was Bob with his slobbery tongue lolling out of his mouth running around on the grass.

I immediately put Operation Get Out Of The Bag into action. I scrabbled around frantically for the magic pine cone and got it around my neck as fast as I could.

"Bob! Bob!" I called.

Bob was totally bamboozled. He looked this way and that.

"Bob!" I cried. "Over here."

Tamsin and her dad were nearly out of the park.

"Come on, Bob! LOOK OVER HERE!"

Finally, he looked around at the backpack bobbing up and down on Tamsin's back. I quickly turned around and stuck my bottom out of the hole in the bag.

Sure enough, as soon as Bob saw it, he went for it!

"ARF! ARF!" he barked as he galloped

towards Tamsin, his teeth gnashing. When he reached the poor unsuspecting girl, he jumped up and tried to bite my backside. Of course, I pulled my botty in just in time and Bob bit the bag instead.

"What the—!" Tamsin and her dad totally freaked out as Bob ripped at the bag with his teeth. Tamsin immediately took the bag off her shoulder and threw it to the floor.

Steve rushed over, waving his arms around. "BOB! BOB! LEAVE!"

"Learn how to control your dog, mate!" said Tamsin's dad as he hid his daughter behind him. It was pretty scary. I MAY have added some more poo and wee to my previous deposits inside the bag. Look, I couldn't help it OK? And I can't help talking about wees and poos.

It's my LIFE. If you don't want wees and poos stuff read another book! Well! Right. Rant over. Back to the story.

"Sorry!" said Steve. "There must be some food in there!"

"Oh right, yeah! Blame me for your mad dog!" screamed Tamsin.

Steve put a lead on Bob and tried to drag him away, but Bob kept his teeth clamped down on the bag. Tamsin's dad pulled the top end of the bag so that he and Bob were locked in a tug of war. Finally, the bag ripped, and I saw my chance. I scampered away and up a nearby tree without anybody noticing. Well, no one except Bob, who barked and frothed at the mouth as he stared up the seemingly empty tree.

"What is wrong with you, boy? Come on!

I'm getting you home. And no treats for you today!"

"You're lucky I don't call the police!" shouted Tamsin's dad as Steve and Bob walked away.

I waved at Bob from the safety of the tree.

"Bye, Bob!" Ha ha! Stupid Bob.

Tamsin picked her bag up off the floor but realised she'd got something stuck on her finger. A small brown oblong.

"Urgh!" she said. "There's poo in my bag. And … why is my pencil case all wet? Someone's pranked me." She stared at her bag in disbelief. "No one pranks me! I prank them!"

"Well, then it serves you right, doesn't it!" her dad said as he tugged her towards the dentist. "Have you been hanging out with those bullies again?"

They went off arguing.

Yes! I thought. Revenge complete!

An eventful day, I think you'll agree? Speak to you tomorrow!

DAY 72

Sorry I haven't spoken much recently but it's been SOOO much fun lately. Merdyn the Wild has gone home, which actually made me sad for a bit. I'll miss the big idiot in a funny sort of way.

So, how can you talk, Bubbles? I hear you ask. Well, guess what? Now Rose can do magic too! Turns out she's related to Merdyn or something, I don't know the details. But that's why he looks a bit like Rose's dad, and why Rose's mum let him sleep in the shed. Anyway, I have my pine cone spell renewed every few days.

I make regular trips to the pet shop, where I have fun insulting people on the bus, and I make Bob's life a misery on a DAILY basis. Generally, my life is pretty good. In fact, I've decided to list the BEST moments of my life – as I've had so many lately – in reverse order:

5) WHEN ROSE BOUGHT ME FROM THE PET SHOP.

4) WHEN MERDYN THE WILD MADE ME ABLE TO TALK.

3) WHEN I POOED AND WEED IN THE MEAN GIRLS' BAGS.

2) WHEN I GOT BOB INTO TROUBLE IN THE PARK.

1) WHEN I FOUND OUT I CARE FOR ROSE.

Yes, I get sad when she gets sad. But then I just try to cheer her up and we both feel better. So it's a WIN–WIN!

Must go now. Need a poo.

MERDYN THE WILD is from the Dark Ages.
He's the world's greatest warlock (don't call
him a wizard), banished to the 21st century
for bad behaviour, and he's about to create a
whole load of trouble for **ROSE**, aged twelve,
and her guinea pig **BUBBLES**.

IF YOU HAVEN'T READ IT
ALREADY, GO BACK AND FIND
OUT WHERE IT ALL BEGAN ...

TURN THE PAGE FOR
THE FIRST CHAPTER!

CHAPTER ONE

FOUL SMELLS AND MAGIC SPELLS

To begin our story, I need you to cast your fertile imagination back to a time that history forgot. No, not the dinosaurs, that's too far . . . no, not the Vikings, that's not far *enough*, and besides, libraries are full of books on those hooligans. No. I want you to imagine THE DARK AGES. The year 511 to be precise, right in the middle of the Dark Ages, which makes it a contender for the darkest year in all of history.

The Dark Ages were called the Dark Ages not because it was always dark (like Iceland in winter) but because nobody REALLY knows what happened during this time. Nobody wrote anything down or took photos (obviously). The Dark Ages were a time full of menace, mystery and, crucially, magic.

Having said all that, one fact I can tell you is that on

a crisp spring night in 511, King Paul and his justice chiefs gathered at a clearing in a forest near the village of Hupton Grey – a place now known as the Oldwell Shopping Centre, near Bashingford, just off the M3 – for the trial of a notorious criminal. The forest looked a lot different back then, of course. The trees were still there for a start, large and imposing, especially when the makeshift court's lanterns cast flickering shadows upon them.

A crowd of around two hundred people had gathered to watch the spectacle about to happen. The smell would have been intolerable to modern noses, as even noblemen didn't bathe for months on end, and most of the audience were peasants, who rarely bathed once in their lifetimes. They elbowed each other and stood on their tiptoes to see the action. You must remember, there was no TV, and no laptops or iPads in those days. For the local folk, this was the equivalent of going to the cinema. Some even brought snacks. Not popcorn of course, but smoked pig snouts and pickled eggs. A trial of a famous criminal such as this was blockbuster entertainment. And what's more, it was in 3D.

"Will the defendant pray riseth!" boomed the

master of ceremonies.

Gasps rippled through the crowd as the defendant rose all right, but not using his feet! Instead he rose, cross-legged, until he was floating some two metres above the ground. His chains tightened around the huge boulder they were fastened to, making a chilling sound: CRINK! And there the famous felon bobbed, like a human-shaped balloon at a birthday party, eyes closed, a playful smile stretched across his filthy face like a schoolboy who knows he's done wrong but couldn't care less. This is the hero – or should I say the *anti*-hero – of our story. His name? Well, you probably read it on the cover of this book, but just in case you missed it, his name is . . . Merdyn the Wild.

King Paul and his chiefs shook their heads. They had hoped that the presence of Evanhart – the King's daughter – might temper Merdyn's mischievous nature. The two had been friends at the School of Alchemy (Magic School to you and me) until, in adulthood, Merdyn chose the path of darkness. Now Evanhart barely recognised the man floating before her, his robes grubby, his beard long and straggly and his hair matted and adorned with stolen trinkets. He looked more like a pirate than a wizard.

"For the prosecution, I calleth Jeremiah Jerabo," boomed the MC.

The smile quickly fell from Merdyn's face. Jeremiah Jerabo had also been at the School of Alchemy, but

Merdyn's memories of *him* were very different from his memories of Evanhart.

Evanhart had been Merdyn's best friend and confidant. Jerabo, however, was a jealous snitch. Every time Merdyn had engaged in anything fun, such as turning the teacher's apple into a toad just as he was taking a bite, Jerabo would tell on him. And here he was, at it again, telling teacher! Except this time it was the King, and there was more at stake than a cane on his backside.

Jerabo swaggered to the centre of the court and cleared his throat like an actor preparing for his big moment. He'd waxed his blond bouffant hair into a point and shaved his yellow beard into a goatee, making his head look not unlike an ice-cream cone.

"Merdyn the Wild!" he piped with great pomposity. "Thou standeth accused of multiple crimes against the

Alchemist's Code. Thou art a thief, a vandal and a mischief maker who knoweth no bounds. Very few of us are born W-blood . . ."

This is probably not a blood group you're familiar with, but in those days, it was quite common, and basically meant being born a wizard or a witch with magical abilities.

". . . and those of us who art, must use their powers for good, like myself and Evanhart. But thou, *Merdyn the Wild* . . ." Jerabo had reached fever pitch – "I putteth it to THEE that thou have become the worst W of all – a *WARLOCK*!"

And I put it to YOU that you're probably wondering why there are so many thees and thous in that sentence. Well, it was the old way of saying you, yours etc. So thou had better get used to it.

The crowd gasped when it heard the word "warlock". Some felt lightheaded, while one or two even fainted and had to receive medical attention. A warlock is basically a bad wizard, times a thousand. They use their magic for nothing but mayhem.

"That's right," Jerabo hissed. "Do thou have anything

to say for thyself, Merdyn the Warlock?"

This was where Merdyn was supposed to defend himself. This was the moment he could have told them where he had put the giant rock he'd stolen from the ancient Magic Circle (he'd carved the face of Evanhart into it and shrunk it to fit in his pocket). He could have pointed out that the gold he had stolen from the royal war chest had actually prevented the King from starting wars, and wasn't that a good thing? He could have made the case for all his actions, but in truth Merdyn didn't care what anyone thought of him any more. So instead, he slowly lowered himself, put his feet upon the ground and announced in a gruff, powerful voice:

"I AM MERDYN THE WILD!
THE GREATEST WARLOCK OF ALL TIME!
DESTROYER OF ENEMIES!
ALL WHO KNOWETH ME DO
BOW DOWN BEFORE ME!

THOU THINKETH THOU CAN CAPTURE ME?"

He let out an almighty howl of laughter.

"THOU MIGHT AS WELL TRY TO SHACKLE THE WIND!"

Never mind gasps, the crowd was now at the part of the movie where they felt genuinely frightened. If there had been a sofa available, they would have hidden behind it. But sofas wouldn't be invented until 1465, so they just closed their eyes instead. It was testament to Merdyn's powers that they felt so scared, even with him chained to a rock the size of Wales.

"Now," said Merdyn in a quieter voice, "if thou will excuseth me, I'll be off." And with that, he opened his tunic to reveal a belt with little leather pouches tied to it. In a flash he took a pinch of herbs from one of the pouches, slapped his hands together – CLAP! – and chanted:

"LYCIUM BARBARUM! GRABACIOUS! THUNDARIAN!"

Thundarian was the name of Merdyn's staff. It had been taken from him upon his arrest, and his plan was to summon it with this spell.

The plan seemed to be working. A great wind swirled around the court and, from behind the chiefs, Thundarian came floating towards Merdyn's outstretched hand. It was a wonderfully gnarled piece of oak around two metres in length, with an intricately carved eagle perched on top.

It was almost in Merdyn's outstretched hand. Had he grasped it at that moment, he would have unleashed all measure of heinous magic on his captors. He would have turned Jerabo to stone, then shattered him into a million pieces with one flick of his finger. He would have turned the King and his chiefs into stinking goats in a thrice. He would have turned on the crowd and magicked their eyes – which were now as big as saucers – into *actual* saucers.

These revenge fantasies were swirling in Merdyn's warped mind as Thundarian got to within millimetres of his straining fingers. But suddenly . . . CRIIINK! Merdyn hadn't realised that there was also a chain attached to his staff. The chain pulled tight, the staff came to a standstill and Merdyn collapsed in a heap, his energy and chance of escape gone.

In the silence that followed came a hearty laugh.

Jerabo had been watching all this with great pleasure.

"I thought thou might try that," he said, and pulled an ornate black and gold spellbook from his tunic. Each witch or wizard had their own way of casting spells and Jerabo, being a stickler for tradition, liked to use a spellbook.

"CASIAN WALLAT FLOATABOAT!"

he muttered, thrusting his hand out, causing Thundarian to drift towards him instead. Then he grabbed Merdyn's precious staff and snapped it over his knee. **CRACK.**

"Nooooooo!' yelled Merdyn.

Even Evanhart winced at this cruelty. She'd seen Merdyn lovingly whittle that staff over hundreds of hours at the School of Alchemy. Merdyn's heart might have closed off over the years, but Thundarian was the one thing he obviously still cared about.

"Curse thee, Jerabo!" Merdyn wailed. "Thou art a scurrilous coxcomb*!"

Jerabo merely chuckled and threw the broken staff

---

*In case you're wondering, scurrilous meant vulgar in the Dark Ages. Coxcomb referred to a cockerel whose 'comb' is a bright red crest on top of its head. Basically, it's a very long-winded way of calling someone a show-off.

pieces down the stone well that stood in the forest clearing. *Tonk, tonk, tink, tonk, tink, tonk, splosh*, went the broken timber. Then he turned to the King.

"I hope this final act of defianceth will convinceth Thy Majesty that we must mete out the very harshest of penalties to this warlock." With great fanfare, Jerabo licked his finger and used it to turn the pages of his spellbook slowly. "The prosecutor recommendeth to the court –"

✳ FLIP – "that he be sent to the Rivers of Purgatory –"

⁺ FLIP ✶ – "for *eternity!*"

The crowd murmured, for they were truly out of gasps by now. Finally, someone was compelled to speak for Merdyn, and that someone was . . . Evanhart.

Everything about Evanhart said 'mellow'. If she were living in the present day, she would no doubt be a yoga teacher, horse whisperer or your favourite auntie. She had long flowing red hair and silver-grey eyes like still pools of calm water.

"Father," she said to the King now. "Please have mercy upon this man. His powers are great. Perchance he could learn to use them for good?"

"'Tis too late for that, Evanhart," spoke the King. "Thy pleas are wasted here."

"Do thou not remember, Father?" Evanhart persisted. "How he did fighteth for thy army in the great war? Brave and fearless was he. Thou said so thyself."

"But Evanhart, that was a long time ago. Since then, he has shown himself a villain time and time again."

"Show him mercy then, dear Father," Evanhart pleaded. "Send him to the Rivers of Purgatory but for a short time only, five years or so . . . Maybe then he will reflecteth and changeth."

"He will never changeth!" bellowed Jerabo. "Why, only last week I was riding my horse and he did turneth it into a chicken! Imagine what a fool I looked riding around on a chicken!"

The crowd couldn't help but laugh when they thought of this. But the King wasn't laughing. He was lost in his daughter's pleading eyes, the goodness radiating from them and clouding his better judgement. Eventually he spoke.

"I have decided," said the King, "that Merdyn be

sentenced to *seven* years in the Rivers of Purgatory."

"Wha—?" Jerabo swallowed before beginning again. "Very well, Thy Majesty," he seethed through his pursed lips. "Seven years in the Rivers of Purgatory it is." With that he turned the pages of his spellbook once again – * FLIP, * FLIP * – and read out the sentencing spell.

"FRANDALIN, BUGANTI, RIVERO. CLOCKASHOCK!"

The court shook for a few seconds before the ground in the centre of the clearing opened up like a giant mouth. A green light shot from the gaping hole and lit up the sky like the aurora borealis. The crowd oohed and aahed as if watching a firework display on Bonfire Night.

On seeing the green light, Evanhart's expression turned even graver. "Father!"

"No more, child!" snapped the King. "Sentence has been passed!"

"But the light. It should not be gr—"

"I said no more!"

The King's men walked Merdyn to the edge of the great hole. For a second, he looked back at the princess.

"Worry not, Evanhart. I shall be back sooner than they knoweth," he said, with a charm that Evanhart recognised at last. But before she could reply, Merdyn was pushed into the glowing green mouth and it snapped shut, causing a mini-earthquake to pulse through the wood.

In the silence that followed, a villager said to his wife, "I'm *definitely* coming to the next one of these."

Evanhart, however, was in no mood for pleasantries. She marched up to Jerabo and grabbed his spellbook.

"Hey! Snatchy Sue!" Jerabo protested.

"Why was there a green light above the mouth of the Rivers of Purgatory?" Evanhart asked, flipping through the book. "It should have been red!"

"How should I know?" said Jerabo. "I don't maketh the rules."

The King looked at his daughter with exasperation. "Why must everything be a *crusade* with thee, Evanhart? *Women are equal to men. Donkeys have the same rights as horses. Rivers of Purgatory should be red and not green!* Must everything be questioned?"

But at that moment – * FLIP, * FLIP * – Evanhart

found what she was looking for. It made her usually rosy freckled cheeks lose their colour entirely.

"'*Clockashock?*' I knew it. 'Twas the wrong spell! Jerabo didn't sendeth Merdyn to the Rivers of Purgatory!"

Voices in the crowd rang out with confused exclamations: "What?" "Another twist?" "I can't take it no more!" All eyes turned to Jerabo, who squirmed like a worm on a hook.

"Oh, didn't I? I'm sure I did," he said. "Although my Latin is a little rusty . . ."

"So, where did he sendeth him?" asked the King.

"To the Rivers of *Time*," said Evanhart softly, her heartbreak obvious to all.

"But what does that mean?" asked the King.

"It means Merdyn is lost. For ever." And Evanhart cast her wide, glistening eyes up to the heavens in despair.

Oh gods, hear Evanhart
plead like a child,
begging for mercy
on Merdyn the Wild.

Happy
World Book Day!

As a charity, our mission is to encourage every child and young person to enjoy reading, and to have a book of their own.

> Everyone is a reader — that includes you!

Whether you enjoy **comics**, **fact books**, **adventure stories**, **recipes** – books are for everyone and every book counts.

On **World Book Day**, everyone comes together to have **FUN** reading. Talking about and sharing books with your friends and family makes reading even more memorable and magic.

Illustration by Allen Fatimaharan © 2021

Where will your **reading journey** take you next?

1 Take a trip to your local bookshop

Brimming with brilliant books and helpful booksellers to share awesome reading recommendations, bookshops are magical places. You can even enjoy booky events and meet your favourite authors and illustrators!

Find your nearest bookseller at booksaremybag.com/Home

2 Join your local library

A world awaits you in your local library – that place where all the books you could ever want to read await. Even better, you can borrow them for **FREE**! Libraries can offer expert advice on what to read next, as well as free family reading events.

Find your local library at gov.uk/local-library-services

Scan here to visit our website!

3 Check out the World Book Day website

Looking for reading tips, advice and inspiration? There is so much to discover at worldbookday.com/getreading, packed with book recommendations, fun activities, audiobooks, and videos to enjoy on your own or as a family, as well as competitions and all the latest book news galore.